99

D1575536

Happy
Birthday
Joey!
You old grey
mare!
♡ you–
Jenna

POOH'S 101 USES FOR A HONEY POT

# Pooh's 101 Uses FOR A Honey Pot

❧ INSPIRED BY A. A. Milne ❧

WITH ILLUSTRATIONS BY Ernest H. Shepard

DUTTON BOOKS
*New York*

It is nice to offer a honey pot to a stranger who appeared on your doorstep in the middle of the night and now wants breakfast. (He may discover that he doesn't like honey, leaving the pot almost full. If so, try to act Sad and Regretful.)

**2** You might try wearing a honey pot as a
protective helmet if you tend to come downstairs
*bump, bump, bump* on the back of your head.

**3** In case of Sudden and Temporary Immersion,
toss the swimmer a corked-up honey pot to use as a float
until you can find a pole with which to fish him out.

**4** If you want to have a picnic by the Pine Trees
but don't have a fair-sized basket, pack your meal
in an empty honey pot instead.

5 At eleven o'clock, when it is
Time-for-a-little-something, the inside of a honey pot
is a good place to look for it.

6 An empty honey pot is a fine place
to store your tea towels if you aren't lucky enough
to have a nice spot to hang them.

**7** Sticking your head in a honey pot is a trick that will greatly amuse some of your friends (though it is likely to frighten others, especially the Smaller Animals).

———————◆———————

**8** A full honey pot can provide you with the energy you need to set off into the cold to sing an Outdoor Song for Snowy Weather.

9 A honey pot makes a fine stand for your umbrellas
(when you are not using them to practice a deception on bees).

10 You might like to crawl inside a honey pot
if you are a small friend-and-relation who has just found
that a whole Expotition is saying "Hush!" to *you*.

**11** A honey pot makes excellent bait
for a Cunning Heffalump Trap. But
before you put it in the trap, make sure
that what it contains *is* honey, right down to the bottom of the jar.
(Somebody may have put cheese in at the bottom just for a joke.)

**12** Dip into a honey pot when that sinking feeling takes
hold in the middle of the night, and you need a snack.

*Some hours later, just as the night was beginning to steal away, Pooh woke up suddenly with a sinking feeling. He had had that sinking feeling before, and he knew what it meant.* He *was hungry. So he went to the larder, and he stood on a chair and reached up to the top shelf, and found—nothing.*

*"That's funny," he thought. "I know I had a jar of honey there. A full jar, full of honey right up to the top, and it had* HUNNY *written on it, so that I should know it was honey. That's very funny."*

*—Winnie-the-Pooh*

**13** When going on an Expotition, carry your provisions in a honey pot. (And then eat them early on, so it won't be too heavy.)

---

**14** If you spot a tasty-looking thistle that you would like to eat later, cover it with a honey pot to keep someone from sitting on it. (Sitting on thistles takes all the Life out of them.)

**15** A large, corked-up honey pot makes
a fine boat. (Remember, you're supposed to sit on *top* of it.)
Paddle vigorously with your feet.

---

**16** If you are short of drawer space, use a honey pot
to store your favorite items of clothing, like mufflers,
shawls, or blue braces.

**17** A full pot of honey is the very best Happy Birthday present.

**18** An empty pot of honey can also be a nice gift,
if you wash it out carefully and
write "A Happy Birthday" on it.

**19** Keep your Strengthening Medicine (and a spoon) in a honey pot and put the pot in a prominent place so that you will remember to take it. (Otherwise, you may grow up Small and Weak.)

—————◆—————

**20** If you have trouble remembering your right paw from your left, simply hold a honey pot in your right one at all times.

**21** If you are a Very Small Animal visiting a friend whose house begins to tilt, you could try to take cover in a honey pot. You may become slightly sticky but are less likely to be hurt when the furniture falls on you.

**22** A honey pot can also hold marmalade, which is nice for breakfast, spread lightly over a honeycomb or two.

**23** If you want to watch the river but are too small to rest your chin on the bottom rail, try standing on a honey pot.

**24** A small honey pot makes an attractive
vase for a bunch of violets.

———————◆———————

**25** Keep a honey pot outside your door
as a mailbox in which to leave important letters
or Missages. If you simply pin a notice
to your door, it may blow off.

**26** A honey pot makes a good helmet if you are standing under a tree from which you fear a Jagular may drop on you.

**27** If you're a Tigger, take a pot of honey with you whenever you climb a tree—in case you can't climb back down because your tail is in the way.

**28**  Always keep a full pot of honey in your cupboard in case someone drops by who would like a mouthful of something.

**29**  When housecleaning, use an old honey pot as a trash can. (If you are helping a friend clean house, ask before you throw anything in it. What you take for a dirty old dishcloth may be a favorite shawl.)

**30**  A honey pot is one of the
first places you could look for a missing
friend-and-relation named Small.

———————◆———————

**31**  If you are surrounded by water
and in need of sending a Missage, a small honey
pot will work as well as a bottle.

**32** When you are in a comfortable position for not listening to Rabbit on a drowsy summer afternoon, dip into a honey pot occasionally to keep yourself from falling asleep.

◆

**33** Count imaginary honey pots when you have trouble falling asleep. This can be very restful, as long as you don't begin counting Heffalumps, too.

*The more he tried to sleep, the more he couldn't. He tried Counting Sheep, which is sometimes a good way of getting to sleep, and, as that was no good, he tried counting Heffalumps. And that was worse. Because every Heffalump that he counted was making straight for a pot of Pooh's honey,* and eating it all.

—*Winnie-the-Pooh*

**34** You might Issue a very large honey pot as a Reward for something you have lost, especially if you were very attached to it.

**35** Use a honey pot to hold hammers, nails, and other tools—you never know when they will come in handy.

**36** Pack your lunch in an empty honey pot. It is sturdier than a bag and will keep your watercress or Extract of Malt sandwiches from getting squashed.

———◆———

**37** Simply thinking about a honey pot is a wonderful way to become inspired to write a Poem or a Hum. Thinking of a *full* honey pot is particularly inspirational.

**38** If you stick your head in a honey pot
and roar, you can make a very loud echoing noise.
Unfortunately, you may have to break the pot to
remove it. (Try banging it against a tree root.)

---

**39** A honey pot is a nice place
to keep string—especially the kind you'll need
to lead Heffalumps home with.

**40** A honey pot is a good place to keep a supply of
thistles, for those gloomy times when you cannot find any
(or when someone has just eaten the little patch you
were keeping for your birthday).

**41** An empty honey pot is a perfect place
to keep balloons before they are blown up—or after
they've been reduced to a small piece of damp rag.

**42** Honey pots can be used to store many other foods in your cupboard, like condensed milk and other teatime favorites.

———————◆———————

**43** Try demonstrating with honey pots if you are having trouble teaching a Bear of Little Brain about Twy-stymes.

**44** Keep a honey pot by your front door
as a step stool, in case a Very Small Friend who
cannot reach the knocker drops by.

**45** For one who often writes Notices or other important Missages, a cleaned-out honey pot can make a Useful inkwell.

**46** Use a honey pot as a desk when signing an important Rissolution, and you will be less likely to smudge.

**47** If you can't find a friend when you need
to pull on your Big Boots, lean against a large honey pot
so you won't keep falling over backwards.

**48** If you'd like to sit in the middle of a
stream that has no stepping stones, wade in with
a honey pot to sit on instead.

49  When you give a special sort of party, serve small pots of honey, which your guests may enjoy just as much as those little cake things with pink sugar icing.

———◆———

50  If you run out of chairs, overturned honey pots can serve as seats for your smaller friends-and-relations.

———◆———

51  After the party, it would be Kind and Thoughtful to put the odd bits which got trodden on into a honey pot and send it down to someone who did not attend.

**52** If you are a small animal walking outside on a very windy day, carrying a full honey pot may keep you from blowing away.

———————◆———————

**53** If you have never been able to count the number of trees in the enchanted place at the top of the Forest, try putting a honey pot by each tree and then counting the pots instead. You will need quite a few: sixty-three or sixty-four at least.

**54** Flying while holding on to a honey pot may help strengthen and develop your Dorsal Muscles.

———————◆———————

**55** When building a house, you could use a big honey pot to collect the sticks you need. (Just make sure that they aren't part of someone's house already.)

**56** Simply count your honey pots if you have nothing else to do. You may find that knowing you have fourteen pots left—or fifteen, as the case may be—is sort of comforting.

**57** Try a taste from a honey pot when you need a little something to sustain you on a warm day.

*It was a warm day, and he had a long way to go. He hadn't gone more than half-way when a sort of funny feeling began to creep all over him. It began at the tip of his nose and trickled all through him and out at the soles of his feet. It was just as if somebody inside him were saying, "Now then, Pooh, time for a little something."*

*"Dear, dear," said Pooh, "I didn't know it was as late as that." So he sat down and took the top off his jar of honey. "Lucky I brought this with me," he thought. "Many a bear going out on a warm day like this would never have thought of bringing a little something with him." And he began to eat.*

*—Winnie-the-Pooh*

**58** The contents of a particularly fine honey pot will comfort you after you discover that instead of tracking Woozles, you have been following your own paw prints all morning.

———————◆———————

**59** Keep your colored pencils, rulers, and India rubber in an empty honey pot if you don't have a Special Case for them.

60 Filled with warm water, a honey pot is
a good place to dunk your tail if it has lost all feeling
from being in a cold stream for too long.

⎯⎯⎯⎯⎯◆⎯⎯⎯⎯⎯

61 A honey pot can be used to carry sand from
the Forest back to your house, so that you can practice
jumps in your very own sandpit.

62 Try talking with your head in a honey pot when you want to disguise your voice, in order to fool unexpected visitors into thinking that you are not at home.

63 You could also try using a large honey pot to block your door, if you would rather not have Company and such like. Remember, guests—especially those who empty the honey pot—may stay Longer Than Expected.

**64** A honey pot is an excellent place
to store your haycorns, whether you are planning
to eat them or plant them around your front
door so they can grow into oak trees.

———————◆———————

**65** Honey pots are equally useful
for storing mastershalum seeds.

66 Use an empty honey pot to carry plates, napkins, and utensils on a picnic. (Of course, you will need a full pot of honey for the picnic as well.)

———◆———

67 A new honey pot is a thoughtful housewarming gift.

**68** Use a honey pot as a nightstand for your candle, which you may need in order to see what's making that *worraworraworra* noise outside your door in the middle of the night.

**69** Lifting a full honey pot (*one, two, one, two*) can be Useful when doing one's Stoutness Exercises.

---◆---

**70** A honey pot is a good place to sit and rest after doing your Stoutness Exercises.

---◆---

**71** A honey pot is also a good source of refreshment following your Stoutness Exercises.

**72** Use a honey pot to store sticks in,
with which you can practice making letters
—if you are Educated, that is.

**73** Practice counting by lining your
honey pots up in a row. But don't try it when
you are expecting a knock on the door
—you may become muddled.

**74** A very small pot of honey is just
the thing to serve at a Very Nearly tea, which
is one you forget about afterwards.

**75** A large pot of honey, on the other hand,
is appropriate to serve at a Proper Tea.

**76** When you feel so Foolish and Uncomfortable that you have almost decided to run away to sea and be a sailor, simply hide your head in a honey pot instead.

— • —

**77** If you are feeling rather motherly and Wanting to Count Things—like vests and pieces of soap—an empty jar of honey is a fine place to put them once they've been counted.

**78** If you want to paint a name over your door in gold letters, an old honey pot is handy for mixing paint or holding brushes.

**79** Always keep some honey pots on hand that are at least partly full for Sustenance in case of an Emergency, such as being surrounded by water.

*"This is Serious," said Pooh. "I must have an Escape."*

*So he took his largest pot of honey and escaped with it to a broad branch of his tree, well above the water, and then he climbed down again and escaped with another pot . . . and when the whole Escape was finished, there was Pooh sitting on his branch, dangling his legs, and there, beside him, were ten pots of honey. . . .*

*Two days later, there was Pooh, sitting on his branch, dangling his legs, and there, beside him, were four pots of honey. . . .*

*Three days later, there was Pooh, sitting on his branch, dangling his legs, and there, beside him, was one pot of honey.*

*Four days later, there was Pooh . . .*                    —*Winnie-the-Pooh*

**80** When you are trying to lose someone
in the Forest, use some small honey pots to mark
your trail so you don't lose yourself.

———————◆———————

**81** If you get lost anyway, be quiet for a moment and listen.
The twelve honey pots in your cupboard may call you home.

**82** Instead of balancing on three legs, lean on a honey pot when you bring your fourth leg up to your ear so you can hear better. This may keep you from falling down again.

---

**83** Bring a small honey pot along as a snack when you go for a walk in the Forest. If you happen to fall into a sort of Pit, you will not go hungry while waiting to be rescued.

**84** If nobody notices it is your birthday, turn a honey pot upside down and pretend it is a cake with candles and pink sugar. Enjoy yourself. (Some can.)

**85** Keep your tail safe in a honey pot while you wait for someone to bother to nail it back on.

**86** A small honey pot is a perfect
place to hide your Strengthening Medicine
if you have a friend who is always taking
large golollops of it from you.

**87** A honey pot is a perfectly proper serving dish.
If you have a nice pot of honey on the table, there is
no need for a bowl or plate at all.

**88** If your house blows down in such a way that
your door is now on the ceiling, try stacking some honey pots
high and climbing them in order to make an Escape.

**89** An empty honey pot can be washed and refilled with a fresh supply of honey, if you can outsmart the bees who make it.

**90** A large, overturned honey pot can be used as a podium when you have something to read aloud, be it a Poem, a Plan, or a Rissolution.

**91** A pot of honey shared with company can turn even a cold and dreary Thursday into a Very Friendly Day.

**92** If you should happen to be a Wedged Bear
in Great Tightness, an overturned honey pot could be used
as a place to rest your head and paws.

———————•———————

**93** In that same situation, a clean honey pot could also
be used to store Sustaining Books and other reading material.

**94** Worn over your face, a honey pot makes a Clever Disguise that may deceive others into thinking that you are a Horrible Heffalump.

**95** If you are trying but failing to distract a Strange Animal by reciting a piece of poetry, try offering her a lick from a honey pot instead.

96 A honey pot is a good place to keep a large supply of Extract of Malt, in case someone comes to live with you who has it for breakfast, dinner, and tea.

**97** Emptying a honey pot will
restore your strength after a long Explore.

**98** A honey pot is a perfect place
to put the fir-cones that you have
gathered for a game of Poohsticks.

**99** If you need to wash someone ashore but cannot find a large stone to drop, a large honey pot will *boosh* him just as well.

**100** A pot of honey would make a nice gift
for someone who is going away, especially if accompanied
by a Poem signed by all his friends.

**101** If you need a friend, open a fresh pot of honey
and wait at the top of the Forest. The Best Bear in
All the World will find you.